Willowbank

Helping Hand

by Alan Fennell

It was very hot. The sun had been shining fiercely for many days and away from the cover of the trees of Moonshine Wood, the earth had become baked and dusty.

Sundown Squirrel and his friend Rainbow Rabbit had found a new game...dust sliding.

Perched on top of a steep bank, Rainbow waited for Sundown to shout "go" and then tried to beat the squirrel to the bottom of the slope.

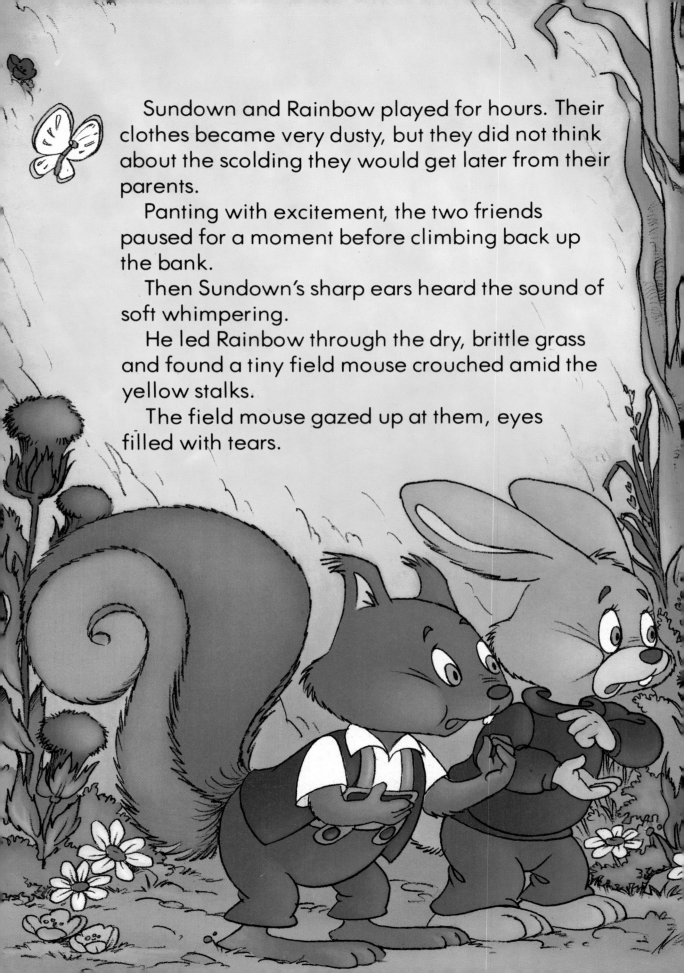

Sundown and Rainbow played for hours. Their clothes became very dusty, but they did not think about the scolding they would get later from their parents.

Panting with excitement, the two friends paused for a moment before climbing back up the bank.

Then Sundown's sharp ears heard the sound of soft whimpering.

He led Rainbow through the dry, brittle grass and found a tiny field mouse crouched amid the yellow stalks.

The field mouse gazed up at them, eyes filled with tears.

"What's wrong?" Sundown asked gently.

"The sun has dried up the grass and the seeds are not nice," replied the field mouse whose name was Busy Feet. "All my relations are starving."

Sundown was puzzled. "Can't you find food in the shade of the forest?" He knew field mice were timid creatures who didn't like to stray too far from their homes, and he had noticed the tall pine trees beyond the field.

"We do usually when it's so hot," replied the pretty mouse. "But Storm the Pine Marten won't let us near the forest."

"We'll soon see about that," said Sundown bravely. "Let's go to the forest."

As they ran and hopped along the tiny pathways cut through the field by the mice, Sundown remembered Storm the Pine Marten. He was a fierce fellow. Not as dangerous as Sharp Fang the Weasel, who was his cousin, but an animal not to be trusted.

The pine forest was not a favourite place of Sundown and Rainbow, for they preferred the friendly folk in Moonshine Wood, and the squirrel and rabbit were cautious as they followed Busy Feet.

Suddenly there was a piercing scream and firm hands grabbed the three youngsters.

Squirming and struggling, they were carried
into the forest by angry looking pine martens.
Beneath a tall pine tree which stretched high to
the cloudless sky, stood Storm.

"I suppose you've come to steal my food," he
snarled. "Good thing I placed guards around the
forest."

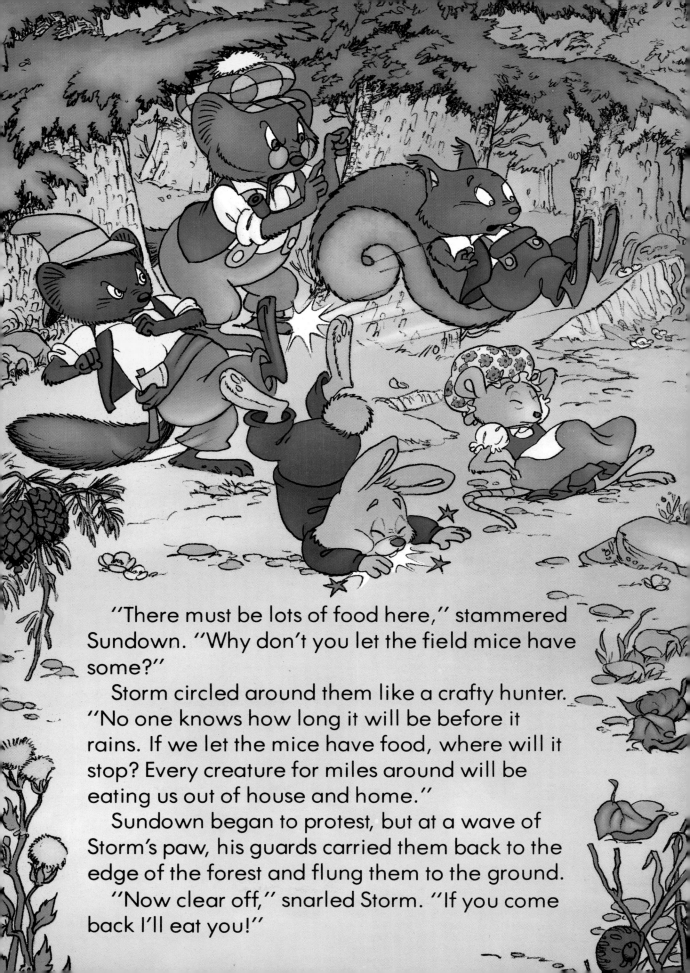

"There must be lots of food here," stammered Sundown. "Why don't you let the field mice have some?"

Storm circled around them like a crafty hunter. "No one knows how long it will be before it rains. If we let the mice have food, where will it stop? Every creature for miles around will be eating us out of house and home."

Sundown began to protest, but at a wave of Storm's paw, his guards carried them back to the edge of the forest and flung them to the ground.

"Now clear off," snarled Storm. "If you come back I'll eat you!"

Busy Feet began to cry again as they scurried quickly away from the tall trees. "I'm so hungry," she sobbed.

Sundown smiled kindly at her. "You'd better come to our village. It's a long way for you to walk, but we have lots of food."

This was true, for Willowbank Glade was a sheltered spot deep in Moonshine Wood and the moist conditions helped the grass and shrubs to grow even when there was a drought.

While Busy Feet ate her fill, and she had a tremendous appetite, Sundown spoke to Grandfather Pen Badger who knew almost everything there was to know.

"You should not be too angry with Storm," said Grandfather Pen. "He is not very intelligent and he is frightened about being invaded by his neighbours."

"You're not frightened about losing *our* food," Sundown said.

"Ah," smiled the badger. "Willowbank is deep in the wood. It is not an easy place to find...and we ration our stores at times like this. We allow a little for everyone and so the food lasts."

Sundown thought it would be a good solution
for Storm to ration the food, but he wasn't going
to be the one to suggest it — he still remembered
the marten's fierce warning

"Come on, Busy Feet," he called to the field
mouse. "Rainbow and I will take you to your
home. You've had more than your ration."

As they reached the edge of the field,
Rainbow's constantly moving nose sniffed at the
air. "What's that horrible smell?" he asked.

Sundown scampered to the top of a hillock and
his tail twitched in alarm.

"Fire!" shouted Sundown. "The forest is on fire!"

Fear gripped the three youngsters. Fire was the most dangerous of all the elements. They did not know what to do next, and not even the sudden appearance of Storm and his family could move them.

"Help us, please help us," cried Storm, shaking in panic. "Our homes have been destroyed and all our food is gone."

So surprised was Sundown at Storm's sad expression he overcame his fright.

"What did you say when Busy Feet and her family asked for help?" Sundown asked sternly.

"I know," agreed Storm. "I've been very selfish. Now it's all gone. What can I do?"

Sundown moved cautiously to Storm's side. He remained wary of the pine marten.

"We'll go to see Grandfather Pen Badger. Perhaps the citizens of Willowbank will help."

When Sundown explained about the forest fire, all the creatures in Willowbank welcomed Storm and his family into their homes.

For many of them it was a tight squeeze and the martens kept bumping into things, but by taking turns to sleep and by rationing food, they all learned the best way to get along.

The drought lasted two more weeks. Then, early one morning, Sundown was awakened by the pit-a-pat of rain on the window. He rushed outside and leapt on to the willowtree stump in the centre of the village.

"Wake up, everyone," he shouted. "It's raining! It's pouring! Come and look...it's wonderful!"

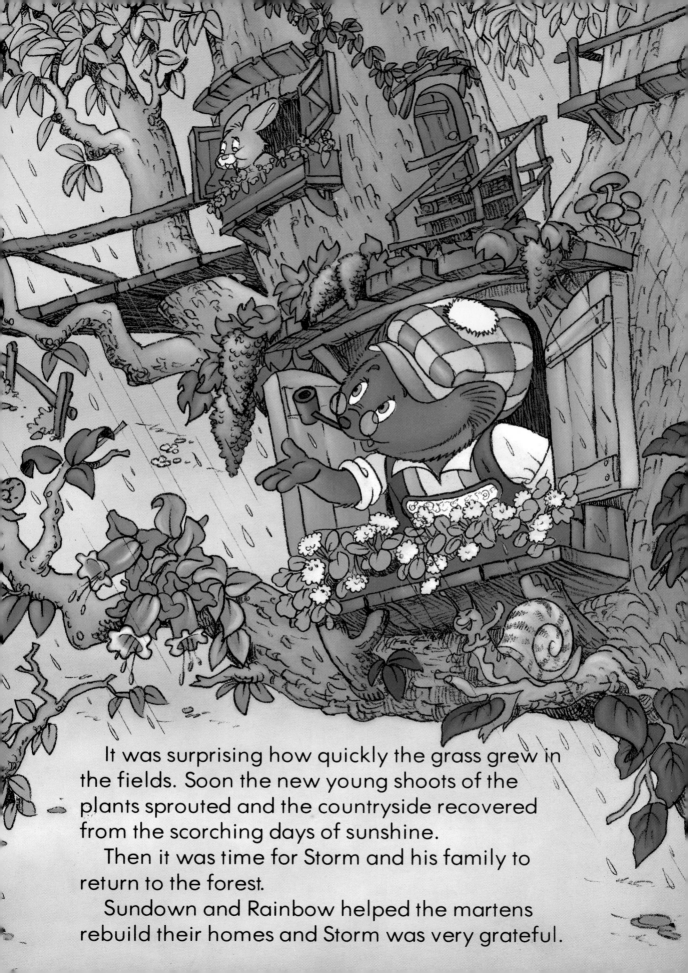

It was surprising how quickly the grass grew in the fields. Soon the new young shoots of the plants sprouted and the countryside recovered from the scorching days of sunshine.

Then it was time for Storm and his family to return to the forest.

Sundown and Rainbow helped the martens rebuild their homes and Storm was very grateful.

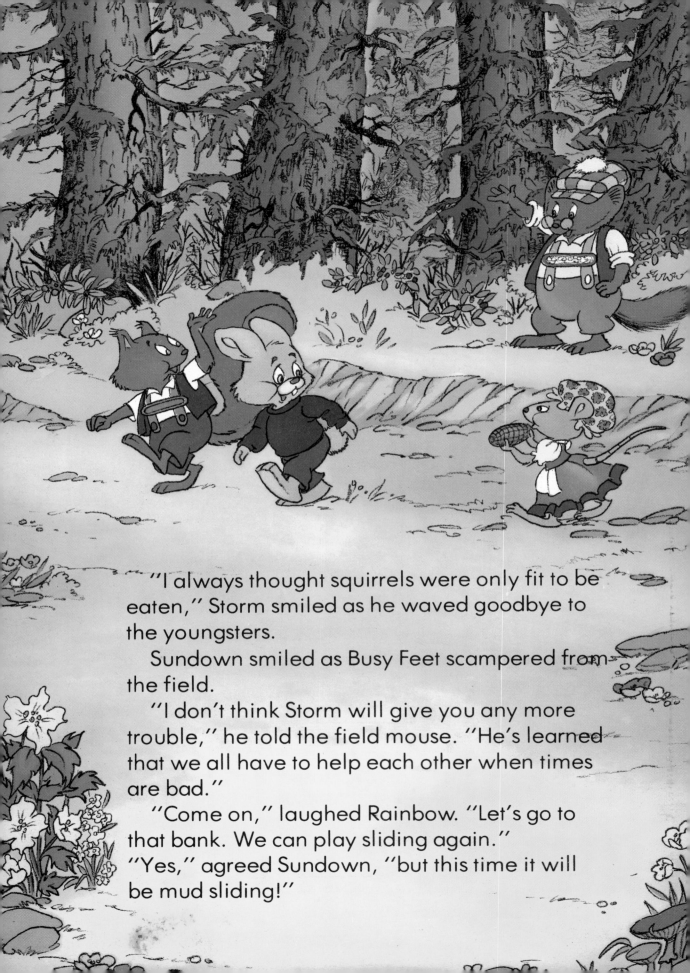

"I always thought squirrels were only fit to be eaten," Storm smiled as he waved goodbye to the youngsters.

Sundown smiled as Busy Feet scampered from the field.

"I don't think Storm will give you any more trouble," he told the field mouse. "He's learned that we all have to help each other when times are bad."

"Come on," laughed Rainbow. "Let's go to that bank. We can play sliding again."

"Yes," agreed Sundown, "but this time it will be mud sliding!"

Willowbank

The Night Raiders
by Alan Fennell

Dark rain clouds hid the moon as the citizens of Willowbank Glade slept soundly through the night. No one heard the rustle in the undergrowth as busy, scampering feet sped through the wood towards the village.

The night raiders were on the prowl.

Strangers to the district, the pack of rats were worthless creatures who did not work for their food. They stole it . . . attacking and gnawing the brightly polished shutters of Mrs Silver Quill's root level cottage.

She was a houseproud hedgehog and the tears would certainly flow when she discovered the assault on her home.

Nothing was safe from the robbers. They broke into many houses in the village, and if anyone heard the rats, no one could stop them, for they were strong and vicious.

The snug hollow where Sundown Squirrel lived with his parents and brothers and sisters did not escape. Mrs Brush Tail, Sundown's mother, was the main supplier of acorns and nuts to the village.

The raiders were delighted to find such rich booty and they chattered and squeaked as they made off with their haul.

Sundown, whose bedroom was above the hut store, heard the thieves and peered cautiously around the door, not quite sure what to do.

He knew he could not stop the rats. They were too powerful for one small squirrel. He waited until they had left Willowbank, then he woke his friend Rainbow Rabbit and set off in pursuit of the raiders. "If we find their hide out," said Sundown "we can think of a way to get back our food."

The rats journeyed deep into the wood but Sundown took carefull note of the paths they travelled.

At last they came to an ugly rubbish dump at the southern edge of Moonshine Wood.

"Shall we go for help now?" asked Rainbow timidly.

"Yes," agreed Sundown. "It will be light soon." Then he had an uneasy thought. "Rats fight hard when they are cornered. I'm not sure if our Willowbank friends will want to tackle them."

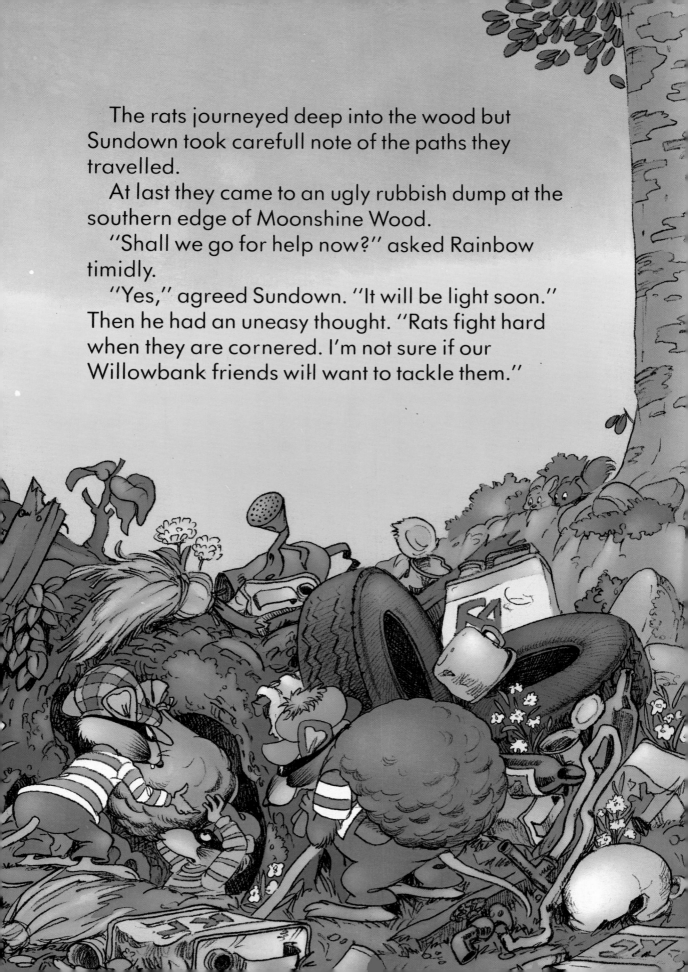

The first rays of the sun were beginning to chase away the night shadows when Sundown had an idea.

"If those rats don't like the taste of Mrs Silver Quill's shutters," he said, pausing in a clearing, "they'll leave them alone."

Rainbow nodded, but did not know what Sundown had in mind.

"And," went on Sundown, "if we can get the nuts to run away from the hideout, perhaps the rats won't steal them again."

"It sounds like a good plan," frowned Rainbow,
"but how do we make it all happen?"

Sundown ran to some large purple flowers.
"Come on, help me collect these petals."

"But we've been warned about these flowers,"
protested the rabbit. "They're poisonous."

"Exactly," laughed Sundown. "Now remember to
wash your hands when we've finished."

When Sundown and Rainbow arrived home, the Willowbank folk were holding a meeting to discuss the robbery.

The squirrel and the rabbit set to work to mix the poisonous petals with paint, and after young Carpenter Mouse had repaired Mrs Silver Quill's shutters, they painted them with the strange solution.

When they had finished, everyone was warned about the dangerous taste of the paint, but poisonous though it was, the violet colour made Mrs Silver Quill's curtains look a real picture.

"Now I'm going to have a word with some friends of mine," decided Sundown.

The next night, the greedy rats returned to Willowbank, and while the villagers watched, the raiders set about Mrs Silver Quill's shutters.

Suddenly, they fell to the ground, rolling about in pain.

"Urgh!" the chief raider groaned. "This wood tastes awful."

"My belly aches," grumbled another.

Doubled up in agony, the robbers struggled from Willowbank and limped home to their rubbish dump.

Sundown and Rainbow followed at a safe distance.

As the rats reached the hideout, they received another shock. All the nuts and seeds they had stolen seemed to be marching away into the wood.

"Hey!" shouted one of the rats, "those are our nuts!"

"I don't like my food walking about," said the rat leader. "I'm going to find somewhere else to raid. Willowbank can keep its rotten wood and walking nuts."

"Horray," cheered Rainbow. "But how did you
get the nuts and fruit to walk?"
"Come and see," chuckled Sundown.

The happy squirrel ran after the nuts with Rainbow hopping along behind. When they had caught up, the nuts stopped and suddenly they rolled to one side to reveal an army of ants.

"Meet my friends," laughed Sundown. "I told you they would help us."

The ant captain gave a smart salute and after winking knowingly at Sundown, gave his soldiers their orders.

"Right, men," he said, "it's a long way to Willowbank. On the command, pick up your loads and quick march."

With straight backs and swinging arms, Sundown and Rainbow fell in behind the soldiers. What a cheer they received when they reached Willowbank.